THE
MIRRORSTONE

MICHAEL PALIN

ALAN LEE

RICHARD SEYMOUR

JONATHAN CAPE
THIRTY-TWO BEDFORD SQUARE LONDON

For Anne

First published 1986

Copyright © 1986 by Richard Seymour, Michael Palin and Alan Lee

Jonathan Cape Ltd, 32 Bedford Square, London WC1B 3EL

British Library Cataloguing in Publication Data

Palin, Michael
The mirrorstone.
I. Title   II. Lee, Alan   III. Seymour, Richard, *1947–*
823'.914[J]   PZ7
ISBN 0-224-02408-6

Holograms by Light Fantastic Ltd, London
Hologram blocking by Blockfoil Ltd, Ipswich
Holographic models by Alan Lee, Ray Evangelista and Wendy Froud

Printed in Great Britain by
Chorley & Pickersgill Ltd, Leeds

he first time he saw it was at the swimming baths. He dried his hair as usual, pulled out his Mickey Mouse comb, glanced in the mirror and then started back in shock. For the face he saw looking back at him was not his own. It wasn't very different, but something was wrong. The hair was a bit longer, the cheeks were a bit thinner. "Do I really look as bad as that?" thought Paul, peering closer. And that's when he got an even bigger shock. For as he moved nearer to the mirror the other face stayed still! Paul felt himself go very cold for a moment, then he heard a shout from one of the boys behind him, "Stop staring at yourself, we all know you're ugly!" When Paul looked at the mirror again, there, sure enough, was his own freckly, friendly face.

Paul was the best swimmer in the school. He was especially brilliant at swimming under water. He could swim three lengths of a pool without once coming up for air. In fact that day Paul had spent such a lot of time under water he wondered if this was why he was seeing things.

The next day something very odd happened again. He was cleaning his teeth when he was aware of a strange sensation, as if he were being watched. He looked up and there was the face that wasn't quite his face staring back at him from the mirror. This time it couldn't possibly be him because Paul had a mouthful of toothwater, and the other face didn't. He smiled as best he could, but the face didn't smile back. Suddenly, the bathroom door flew open and his mum rushed in looking for her ear-rings.

"Are you all right?" she asked,

"You look as though you've seen a ghost."

Paul shook his head.

"No…no…I'm fine." he muttered. As soon as his mother had gone he looked back into the mirror. There was nothing there except a schoolboy – with a blob of toothpaste on the end of his chin.

After school that day Paul was walking home past the old T.V. repair shop when he stopped in amazement.

Usually he didn't notice the T.V. repair shop. It was always closed and all the televisions inside were broken anyway but today something was different. One of the old television sets seemed to be on.

He pressed his nose up against the window. What he saw made him suddenly stiffen. The television wasn't actually on at all.

It was a reflection on the screen.

He could see the cars passing in the road behind him, but where he should have been was the boy from the mirror.

Paul jumped back and for a moment he saw the face reflected on every dusty screen in the shop.

He turned and ran.

He dropped his schoolbag, caught his foot in it, and falling headlong onto the road, was nearly run over by a 24 bus.

It screeched to a halt and Paul picked himself up and walked on, trembling.

When Paul reached home, instead of throwing his bag at the cat and switching on the television, he threw himself at his mother and clung on to her.

"You're old enough to know about crossing the road, Paul, honestly." He held on to her even harder.

"I saw something…in the shop…"

"*Seeing* things! Now come on, you're just shaken up and a good thing too. You'll be more careful next time."

Paul decided to tell her everything, about the faces, about the boy he kept seeing. But she was in a hurry as usual.

"I'll be back at half-past. I'll bring a McDonald's. Be good."

A moment later he heard the door slam.
The flat was very quiet.
He sat down until he could feel his heart beating more slowly.
His knee hurt. Looking down he saw a long dark graze.

There was even a smear of blood. He went into the bathroom, switched on the light and pulled open the door of the cupboard where the medicines were kept.

He heard a noise.

At first he thought it was the squeak of the cupboard door.

Then it came again.

This time there was no mistaking it. It was a voice yet there was no one else in the house.

It was coming from the direction of the mirror.

Other voices joined in. Paul turned slowly towards the mirror and there was the boy.

"What do you want?" cried Paul.

The boy said nothing but stretched out his hand as if beckoning Paul to follow him.

"Where are you going to take me?" asked Paul, trying to keep his voice from shaking. He followed the boy closer to the mirror, and as he did so an icy breeze blew into the bathroom, although it had no window, and the sound of the voices grew. The bathroom he knew so well began to disappear, the light became brighter, the wind blew stronger and the next moment Paul found himself, blinking, in the middle of a strange city. It was full of towers topped with flags which swirled in the breeze. He recognised nothing and no one. It was like a picture in a history book. He looked behind him, but there was no sign of the bathroom. He looked ahead of him, but there was no sign of the boy.

The voices he had heard belonged to a crowd of people who had gathered and were staring at something in a most unfriendly way. Then he realised that what they were staring at was him. He followed their eyes down to the tips of his white training shoes with the holes in the toes and up past the dirty old jeans to the faded Ghostbusters T-shirt which his mother was always trying to throw away, and he suddenly understood just why they were staring. They'd never seen anyone looking like him before, and they didn't seem to like it.

"Hey you!" A most evil-looking man stepped forward and came up so close to Paul that he could see bits of cheese in his beard…"You're coming with us!"

Paul realised that the only brave thing to do was to run away, and without knowing quite where he was going he raced across the square, through a fountain, scattered a flock of geese, ducked under a balcony, and disappeared down a narrow passage. He could hear shouts behind him, getting closer and closer. He caught sight of some stairs leading to a lighted window high up above him and threw himself desperately towards them. The stairs seemed to go on for ever and he was breathing in great gasps as he reached the top and squeezed himself into a darkened doorway. Then the door he was leaning against fell open and he tumbled into a cluttered cobwebby room, in the middle of which sat a very old man indeed.

"Ah, *there* you are! We've been waiting for you."

he man's hair was long and matted as though it hadn't been washed for years. His face was lined and wrinkled, as if he'd been through a dozen lifetimes, but the eyes that stared at Paul were bright and piercing. Paul was still gazing at him when he felt himself being pulled into the room, his clothes were wrenched off and a thick itchy brown tunic was thrown over his head. He winced as his arm was twisted behind his back and he was pushed up close to the old man.

"Mary! Don't be so rough with him!" cried the old man.

Turning his head to see who was holding him so tightly, Paul was amazed to find himself looking into the face of a girl, not much older than himself. She looked scornfully down at him as she dropped his faded Ghostbusters T-shirt into the middle of the fire.

The old man nodded at the girl and she released Paul. She reached onto a table full of books and bottles and maps and skulls and picked up a pair of spectacles with very thick glasses which she put on the old man, so that when he looked at Paul his eyes seemed to have grown four or five times bigger. Paul felt that they were staring right through him. The old man looked him up and down. "Yes…yes…you're just the boy we want, Paul…*just* the boy we want."

"How did you know my name?"

"I know everything."

"If you know everything," said Paul, "then where's the boy who brought me here, the boy in the mirror?"

"Oh, you'll find him," said the old man with a thin smile. Paul looked around the room.

It was small and full of measuring instruments, maps, stuffed animals and old timepieces.

Near the window was a telescope of sorts, pointed up into the sky and beside it a table covered with so many books that it looked to Paul like at least forty-two years' homework.

"You'll find him when you've done what you're here for."

"What am I here for?" asked Paul, trying to sound brave, and failing miserably.

The old man raised his head impressively.

"Let me tell you. My name," he said grandly, "is Salaman." He seemed a bit cross when Paul said "Who?" and he muttered something rude about the way history was taught.

"I am, in my humble way, a genius. I have spent my lives studying glass, reflections…mirrors… the movement of light on surfaces, and I have in my researches discovered the formula for the perfect mirror. A mirror that would show people themselves as they really are. Outside *and* inside." His eyes fixed on Paul. They shone fiercely.

"Have you ever seen yourself as you really are? With all your innermost thoughts and feelings visible? So you can never lie to yourself again?"

Then his eyes clouded over as he went on.

any years ago, in the city in which I used to live, I made such a mirror. It was small, no bigger than a large pebble. I called it the Mirrorstone. When the king of the city heard of it, he called me to his court and made me his chief magician though I prefer to be called a scientist. But he didn't want *me*. He wanted the Mirrorstone. I knew he would use it only to dominate people, not to increase his understanding of them.

So I hid the stone from him, and the king swore that if he could not have it, no one should.

He ordered the city's walls to be destroyed and the Mirrorstone was swept away by the sea. But thanks to Mary's father…"

"*Grand*father," said Mary.

"Yes, of course…I forget how old I am…thanks to him I escaped with my life and since then I have been searching for the Mirrorstone every waking hour. And at last I have found it!" With that he lifted a cloth and suddenly the room was full of light. It came from a globe, smaller than a football.

Paul stared open mouthed.

"Look in here!" cried Salaman in triumph, and drew Paul to his side.

What he saw in the globe was an underwater world, as clearly as if he were there himself, and in the centre of it all was a jagged black rock at the very edge of which he could see a luminous stone.

"More light!" ordered Salaman. As Mary held a lamp above the globe the stone began to shine so vividly that it seemed to rise up out of the sea towards them.

"I could touch it!" gasped Paul, "I could hold on to it *now!*"

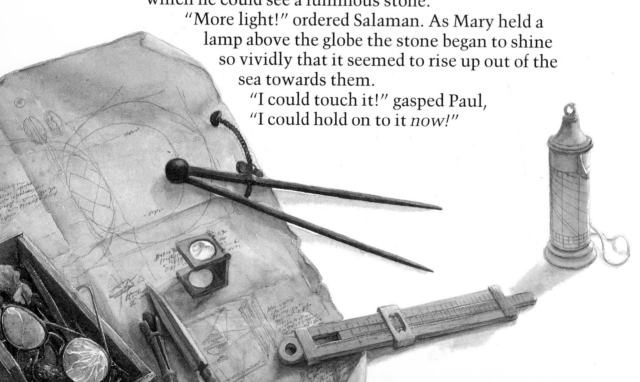

Why don't you try?" suggested Salaman. Paul reached for the stone and his hands closed around it, but he couldn't hold it. He tried again, but once more it slipped through.

"You will be able to touch it soon," said Salaman and turned his piercing gaze once more on Paul.

"Why do you think I wanted a boy who could swim three lengths without once coming up for air?"

"How did you know I could swim three lengths?"

"I told you, I know everything."

Paul felt a strange chill of fear.

There was something in the old man's smile that was only half friendly.

"And now it's time for you to go," he said.

"Go where?" Paul could feel his heart beating faster.

"Don't worry," said Salaman. "I shall guide you there." But he didn't say anything about coming back.

He beckoned Paul towards the luminous globe. Paul looked at the door, but as he did so, he felt Mary's arm very firmly on his. She held him fast. Then he had a surprise, for instead of leading him to the globe, she pulled him towards her and hissed in his ear.

"Escape…now!" Paul stared back at her.

Mary squeezed his arm again.

"You will never come back alive with the Mirrorstone!"

"I can swim…I can swim three lengths without…"

"It's not the water that is the danger, Paul. There are other dangers, far worse."

"What *other* dangers?" Before she could reply Salaman shouted impatiently from beside the globe.

"Paul!" Mary pushed him towards the door.

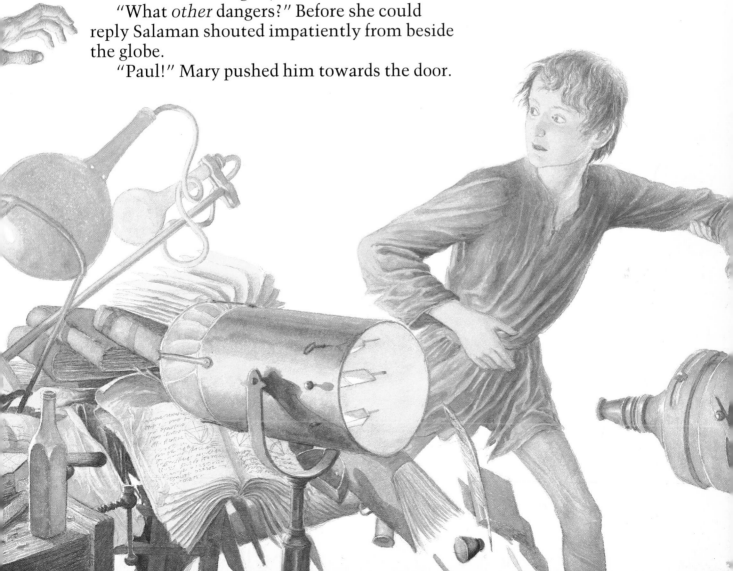

R un!" she screamed.
"Mary!" Salaman's voice was full of anger.
And Paul ran.
Ran for dear life, jumping down the stairs to the street, two or three at a time. Running as fast as he could through the narrow streets, while Salaman's voice shrieked high above him.

Paul raced on, looking neither left nor right, fearing that if he so much as caught a glimpse of a window, a glass or a mirror, Salaman might be there. The voice of the old man grew fainter until it disappeared altogether. It was a long time later, as Paul ran down a rain-soaked alleyway, that he first dared look around him, and he never noticed the gleaming puddle until it was too late.

As his foot touched it he felt, with a terrible sense of helplessness, that he was sinking.

To his horror the puddle seemed to be bottomless and though he kicked and splashed frantically the water rose around him. His hands clawed the sides but he could not save himself and soon he was completely submerged. He felt himself being sucked under and there was nothing he could do but hold his breath as he was pulled down and down.

Then quite suddenly the turbulent water of the
whirlpool gave way to a green and clear calm
and there beneath him was the most
extraordinary sight.
It was a ruined city,
more beautiful
than anything
he'd ever
seen.

e swam on down across seaweed-covered towers and broken battlements. Fish glided lazily out of chimneys and crabs scuttled across disused courtyards. The peacefulness and beauty of it all soothed his fear. What had Mary been so worried about? This was the greatest adventure anyone could have, and he was the luckiest boy in the world!

Paul found himself before the huge doorway of what looked like a royal palace. He swam inside doing somersaults along the corridors and floating through a room where a throne stood empty, its golden legs encrusted with barnacles. This room led into a tower and Paul swam up the narrow stairs faster and faster, until, spinning round like a top, he burst out into the sunlight above the waves. Then he found himself in a room with a table laden with food and he sat down, thinking, "I must be in Paradise!" But there was something strangely familiar about the room. In one corner was a telescope and by the window were piles of books and papers and bottles and skulls. Paul suddenly realised where he'd seen a room like this before. At Salaman's house. "Still trying to escape me?" He turned and there, filling one window, was the unsmiling face of Salaman himself.

aul, this is not the end of your journey." And as
Salaman's face disappeared, a huge wave smashed
across the tower and swept through the room.
Though Paul tried to hang on, he found himself
being washed out and into the sea again. This time
he sank down deeper and deeper, deeper than he'd
ever been before but as the sea cleared he made out far beneath
him the rock he had seen in the globe and beside it the shining
Mirrorstone. If he swam hard he might just reach it, though he was
already deeper than three swimming pools on top of each other.
With a gigantic effort he swam down and at last his feet touched
the rock. Placing them firmly on its pitted surface, he edged slowly
closer and closer until, stretching himself to his limit, his hand
reached the stone.

He'd done it!

ut as he looked into the stone there was no reflection of the shoals of fish and filtered sunlight around him. All he could see was a darkness deep and threatening. He turned and as he did so the rock moved beneath his feet. He felt himself sliding backwards along its rough black surface, struggling to keep his balance. Then as he looked down his heart went suddenly cold. He was staring not at the surface of a rock but into the centre of an enormous eye!

The pupil of the eye widened, then narrowed and Paul could see himself reflected in it, white and shaking with fear.

Gripping the Mirrorstone tightly, he flung himself away as the eyeball seemed to expand and grow red and angry. He looked behind him. The whole rock

was alive! It began slowly to uncoil itself into
something enormous and glistening and scaly.

What had seemed to be solid stone parted
to reveal teeth as strong and hard as rock itself.
As the thing awoke it began to hiss and the water
all around swirled and frothed. Paul desperately
kicked upwards, heading for the surface.

The creature's jagged claws shot out and
caught fast in his tunic. He twisted and kicked and writhed and
struggled. Looking up, the surface of the sea seemed a million
miles away.

He felt himself sinking, his lungs bursting. But he *was* the best swimmer in the school and he gave one last mighty push, his tunic ripped and the claws of the rock creature slipped from him.

Paul shot to the surface and burst out of the water. He never knew fresh air could taste so good.

He tried to swim but he found he could hardly move. There was something stopping him.

He put his hand up to push against the unseen force.

He turned one way and then the other. Paul realised with a sinking heart that he was trapped.

He was surrounded by glass. And outside the glass was a face he recognised only too well.

Salaman screamed in triumph as he held high the crystal ball in which Paul squirmed and wriggled. "My plan has worked! Mary, I *am* a genius!" Mary could see Paul struggling and she knew he had little strength left.

"Let him go, please let him go!" Salaman pushed her to one side.

"Not until I see the stone," he cried. Paul clawed his way helplessly around the slippery sides of the globe.

"He'll die!" shouted Mary. "Send him back where you brought him from before it's too late!"

"Show me the stone!" Salaman screamed and Paul, with the last ounce of his strength, unclenched his fist and pressed the Mirrorstone to the side of the glass. But as Salaman stared into it the look of triumph drained from his face. What he saw in there was not the face of a genius. All he saw was a very old man whose face was lined and wrinkled as if he had lived a dozen lifetimes. He started back with a sharp cry of disappointment and as he did so the globe slipped from his fingers and rolled onto the table.

ary!" shouted Salaman, "The Mirrorstone!"
But Mary did nothing.
The globe rolled the length of the table, halted
momentarily at the edge and as Salaman leapt to save
it, toppled over and hit the ground with a tremendous
crash of splintering, shattering glass. Paul felt himself
hurtling through the air and a moment later he was lying in a heap
on his bathroom floor.

He lay there gasping for breath, his heart beating like a
sledgehammer. He heard the sound of a key in the door, and a light
went on in the hallway.

"Paul?"

Never had he been so happy to hear his mother's voice. He wanted to run to her but he hadn't the strength to move. He heard her footsteps cross the sitting room and at last she pushed open the bathroom door. She didn't seem nearly as pleased to see him as he was to see her. She stared open mouthed first at the mirror and then at Paul.

"What *have* you been doing?" He looked down at the torn, bloodstained tunic Mary and Salaman had given him and he knew that no matter how much of the truth he told, he would never be believed.

"Only a dressing-up game," he mumbled.

"Dressing-up game!" She bent down and pulled him up. "Just look at you!" She turned him towards what was left of the mirror. And this time, when Paul smiled at his reflection, the face in the mirror smiled back.